MMS LMC

Thoughts on this book...

NIGHT GUARD

Written by SYNNE LEA

Illustrated by STIAN HOLE

Translated from the Norwegian
by John Irons

EERDMANS BOOKS FOR YOUNG READERS

GRAND RAPIDS, MICHIGAN / CAMBRIDGE, U.K.

SYNNE LEA is a Norwegian author. She has published two collections of poetry and a young adult novel, which was nominated for the German Youth Literature Prize. She currently works for the Norwegian Institute for Children's Books.

STIAN HOLE is a Norwegian author and illustrator. His previous books include *Anna's Heaven*, *Garmann's Summer*, *Garmann's Street*, and *Garmann's Secret*, all of which were published by Eerdmans. *Garmann's Summer* won a BolognaRagazzi Award and a Batchelder Award Honor.

First published in the United States in 2016 by
Eerdmans Books for Young Readers,
an imprint of Wm. B. Eerdmans Publishing Co.
2140 Oak Industrial Dr. NE
Grand Rapids, Michigan 49505
P.O. Box 163, Cambridge CB3 9PU U.K.

www.eerdmans.com/youngreaders

Originally published in Norway in 2013 under the title
Nattevakt
by Cappelen Damm, Oslo, Norway

© 2013 Cappelen Damm
English language translation © 2016 Eerdmans Books for Young Readers

Manufactured at Tien Wah Press in Malaysia

22 21 20 19 18 17 16   9 8 7 6 5 4 3 2 1

ISBN 978-0-8028-5458-2

A catalog listing is available from the Library of Congress.

This translation is published with the support of NORLA, Norwegian Literature Abroad.

FSC
www.fsc.org
MIX
Paper from
responsible sources
FSC® C012700

Just say
if you need a friend.

If I were you,
I would call out
for me.

I'm not scared
of the dark or of Mom
when she's asleep, of cars that suddenly brake
outside the house. I'm not scared of dreams
in the daytime, of spending the night deep in the forest.
I'm not scared when my little brother bites
his lip till it bleeds. I'm not scared of swallowing
cobwebs or betting
with enemies, or when Dad slips up.
So it doesn't matter, does it,
if I'm a little bit scared
of you?

Because clouds look like something,
are they dreams?

Because dreams exist,
do clouds look like something?

All you need is a friend now
and you're big enough

to walk home alone
in the evening, Dad says.
Then you'll learn

how to rip up the dark
with your hands and throw it at anyone
you think is following you.

Everyone loves little brother.
His soft skin, his light hands.

It's only Grandma who says no,

thanks all the same, to a hug
when his nose is all snotty.

Monsters
don't exist. But under my bed
lives an old lady.

Every evening she asks

for a bit
of my life.

Today it's Mom who is standing
in the garden. If you feel sad, she says,
maybe it'll help you

to know that the trees notice it.
Their spiky branches ache.
They never wish more strongly

that they were soft and more
alive, warm

and had wet noses with just the
right amount of moisture.
They'd like to creep into
the hollow of your neck
and be comforted by
comforting you.

One day when you come for a climb,
the trees also feel that it's fine

to be friends
who just stand there, stretched out
and without feet.

Days will always come when best friends are
those who don't go away.

A warm little
puppy, one who whimpers when he sleeps
in my bed. If not
a warm little puppy, a dog who's
a bit wild, who jumps up
when he sees me, one who bites
my hands only a tiny bit
too hard. A stray dog, one who no one
misses. If not, a dog who hopes for something,
a big dog with a stiff walk and bristly fur,
a lame dog, one who's soon
going to die — soon,
but not quite yet.

No one ever catches
hold of a mom, says Dad. Moms
move quickly — it's
impossible to grab them.
Only if you

sit perfectly still
for a long time,
Dad says, then

perhaps the mom will come
and eat out of your hand. You can try
with an eagle too. Or
a bear.

No, Dad, I say,
Mom moves

like a white anemone —
that gently.

Grandma says
there are streets that feel
they don't fit

names such as Henrik Ibsen, or
Queen Maud, and certainly not
Roald Amundsen Street.

When strangers come and ask them
who they are, they smile and reply
Charlie or
perhaps Betty.

Then they wave and long
to accompany
those who start going the
wrong way.

Henrik Ibsen was a 19th-century Norwegian poet and playwright.

Queen Maud ruled Norway with her husband, King Haakon VII,
in the early 1900s.

Roald Amundsen was a Norwegian explorer and leader of the first
expedition to reach the South Pole.

Who will unlock
the door and let me
in, who will remember
my birthday and plan the summer, who will know
what I like to have
on my bread, who will listen to me
when I sing along
with the others and go ahead of me
in the ski track? Who will warm up
my food and dry between my toes
when I've had my evening bath?
Who will look at me
when I'm asleep? Who will
feel sad when I cry?

Look at me, I say, look at
me when I'm asleep.

What do you think
came here first, the house
or the sky, Mom asks.

When we go into the shop,
she laughs
and asks for a door out

into the open air.
It's all right, she says, we'll travel
just like the rain.

The morning I find
an injured bird, I learn to fly.
Then the summer is down there

far below me. For a short time

all birds
are injured when I find them.

Grandma talks
about the time she was young
and hungry.

I used to love almost
everything, she says, but now
there's only you
I like a bit.

She wants me to tell her
about the way here — birdhouses, curbstones, and if
anyone followed me.

Today our dog doesn't have a name.
No one can call him in.

He stands at the door, waiting
for someone to

throw the summer for him, so he can
run off and fetch
me the sun.

When Mom cries, she cries only
because she's happy, Dad says.
It's when she smiles

it's impossible
to know what she's thinking.

Just go ahead and cry, Dad says, go ahead
and cry. But I don't cry

when I may — I wait
for a time it doesn't fit.

When Mom's asleep,
she isn't

Mom anymore.

If you stand in the forest and think
the trees are breathing in time with you,

it's only because
they stand close

to your window at night and wonder
if they too have to breathe

to be allowed to sleep
along with you.

Can you remember what else
I'm called other than mom,

Mom asks. I nod and clamber up
into the big bed. She tucks
the duvet tightly around me
and tells me to sleep

where her dreams have been
before me. When I was little, Mom whispers,
there were grown-ups

who called out: We're coming to get you.
There still
are, I answer.

If we open the window
and wait long enough, Mom says,
the pigeons will fly in
and pick up everything
we have lost

from the floor, clear up, and give us back
what's lovely and what's nasty
in two bowls. Can you
believe that?

The house hides in the garden,
and the garden tells no
secrets.

I'm the only one who knows

how small the dog gets
in autumn and under
which rosebush Dad has buried
the hair he's lost, the old
map of the world, and Grandpa's
best pair of shoes.

Perhaps the birds too are despondent,
maybe they have a cold and dream
like we do, Mom says. Even so

don't imagine that they're thinking
of you, even though you're
thinking of them.

As long as there's the wind,
Mom says. And the larks when they soar
so lightly. And the mackerel, the moors with swamps
and memories, and sore
feet.

As long as there's you
and me and you and me
and little brother.

Or the kite if it's you
holding it

at the end of a string
that's at least three hundred feet long,
little brother says.

If you take one oar
and I take the other, Dad says,
the boat will gently head toward the shore
while you

think of your friend and I think of
how briefly the two of us will

get to row straight
ahead together.

I know why the winter
doesn't want to go home.
It's lonely

to have to leave just before
the party starts.

The winter wants so much
to say something too,
but doesn't manage to.
So it just stands there
holding heavy snow up
in front of it.

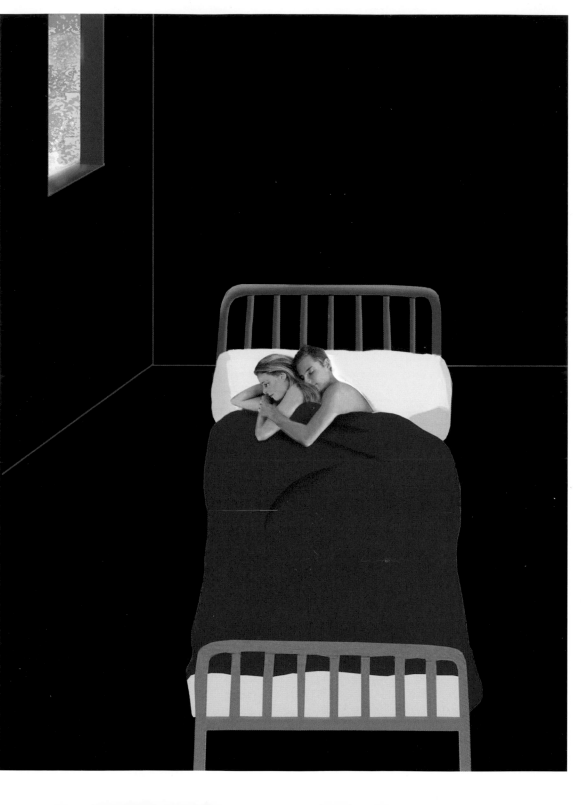

You can hold onto the dog,
Mom says, but you can't choose
what name to give your friend, or how
you'd most like him to play. He's sure to

end up different from what
you imagine. And the same applies
to you too.

We believe that spring is unhappy
every time it gets dark and cold.
That's why it stands out in the green

rain until late at night
and carefully lets birds out
of the winter.

The spring wants to know what it feels like
to be held onto. It is quite sure
how nice it must feel
finally

to be set free
so it doesn't ask about that.

When you've got a friend,
you've always got someone

who insists on lying closest to the wall and will constantly
fall asleep before you do, I tell little brother. You've just
got to try and get used to that the best you can.

When little brother has to learn
how to fall down stairs, I paint
his legs red.
Then the stairs understand at once
they've got to be careful.
Little brother is pleased. He likes his legs
a lot more now. They gleam
when he runs, and when he dances
the floor bows to him
and cries.

That's okay, little brother says
and looks down.

The moon doesn't hold anything,
only lifts off some

of the weight
so you can fly in peace through the night.
But it's not the moon's fault
if you fall

in front of everyone — and not
your fault either.

To sleep is
to wish for something, Dad says.

Awake, you might
find it, says Mom.

If you sit perfectly still and look
very carefully, Dad says,

you may catch sight of birds
migrating through the house. Often the living room
grows dark with crows, but today I think

the swans are coming
with their huge wingspans. Occasionally

something falls down and breaks
when they pass through the kitchen.
Do you think it's strange
that everything still seems
just as whole afterward?

But I quickly notice
that nothing can be used
as before any longer.

Now I'm off, Mom says, now
I'm leaving for where

it's summer. No more
long underwear, ugly shoes, or chapped hands.
I see her walking

down the street in her yellow sandals.
She'll be back, I say, it isn't only
the summer that is warm. Just
feel me.

I can understand
that you like him

because he's happy, Dad says. And because
he bares his teeth at strangers, Mom says.

But that's not the
reason. I like the dog
because he's here.

When Dad leaves,
Mom lights light after light
until the darkness

becomes smaller than us.
At night a lamp is a promise, she says,
the rooms are bonfires, and we

can be beacons. Just think how nice it'll be
when someone doesn't pass

by, but stops
and needs us.

There are trees
that hardly think at all.
They just stand there swaying
exactly as much
as the wind makes them.

And then there are trees
that think all the time.
On some days
it's just a question
of knowing the song.

Today the house is a small
sweater Mom
can't quite pull over her head.
She gives up

and wants me to be
her house. In me there's always
a nice smell, the right warmth, and lots
of space above your head.

Now you must hurry
to work, Mom says
when other moms say: Sleep
tight, sweet

dreams. It's my dreams
I'm not
allowed to play hooky from.

Am I awakened
by you because I'm dreaming
of me?

First my friend
laughs, and afterward
I do.

Then the laughter is
precisely long enough.
I can wind it
three times around my neck,
and get it to warm me
half the winter.

Some days the
windows and doors are wide
open when we come home.
You can just walk

right in. Other days
no keys seem to fit.

If it lasts too long,
I pick the lock. I know why
no one wants to be left alone
too long.

When you pull the kite down,
it isn't the only thing that comes
toward you. Can you also feel

the night getting closer,
and the autumn, high up there?

Can you hear
the school bell ringing? Soon

the kite is a butterfly
in your stomach.

Say something,
so I can see you,
my friend calls out

and asks me if it felt
great to be found.

But I only want to know
how it felt
to find me.